Very Hairy Bear

Alice Schertle

Illustrated by Matt Phelan

Harcourt, Inc.

Orlando   Austin   New York   San Diego   Toronto   London

www.HarcourtBooks.com

Library of Congress Cataloging-in-Publication Data
Schertle, Alice.
Very hairy bear/Alice Schertle; illustrated by Matt Phelan.
p.   cm.
Summary: Recounts the experiences of a shaggy, "boulder-big" bear
as the four seasons come to the beautiful wood which is his home.
[1. Bears—Fiction.   2. Seasons—Fiction.]   I. Phelan, Matt, ill.   II. Title.
PZ7.S3442Ve   2007
[E]—dc21   2003005888
ISBN 978-0-15-216568-0

H G F E D C B

Printed in Singapore

The illustrations in this book were done in pastel and pencil on Rives BFK paper.
The display type was set in P22 Peanut.
The text type was set in Cheddar Salad.
Color separations by Colourscan Co. Pte. Ltd., Singapore
Printed and bound by Tien Wah Press, Singapore
Production supervision by Christine Witnik
Designed by April Ward

To Jen and Drew
John and Kate
Spence and Dylan
   —A. S.

For Rebecca
   —M. P.

Deep in the green gorgeous wood
lives a boulder-big bear
with shaggy, raggy, brownbear hair
everywhere...

except on his
no-hair
nose.

Each spring,
when the silver salmon leap into the air,
fisherbear is there

to catch them.

He stands in the river
with his brown coat dripping.

A very hairy bear
doesn't care
that he's wet.

Kerplunk!

He'll even dunk
his no-hair nose.

In it goes
when he smells *fish!*

Each summer,
he's a sticky, licky honey hunter,
with his bare nose deep
in the hollow of
a bee tree.

A very hairy bear
doesn't care
about stings and things.

Even on his no-hair nose.

When the summer blueberries
grow round and fat on their bushes,
a very hairy bear
doesn't care
that his nose gets blue.

He eats the berries and the bushes, too.
He's a very full
berryfull bear.

In the fall,
when quick gray squirrels hide acorns
under the oak trees,
a no-hair nose knows
where to find them.

A very hairy bear
doesn't care
if the squirrels scold.

He eats all the acorns
he can hold.

Then,

when soft white snowflakes start to fall
and cling to bear hair...

(if there's a bear there),

when fish sink to sleep deep in the pond,
wrapped in their silver scales,

and swarms of bees sleep
deep in their warm honey hives,

and squirrels lay curled
on heaps of nuts
in hollow trees,

he scratches his big brown bear behind
on the roughest tree trunk he can find,

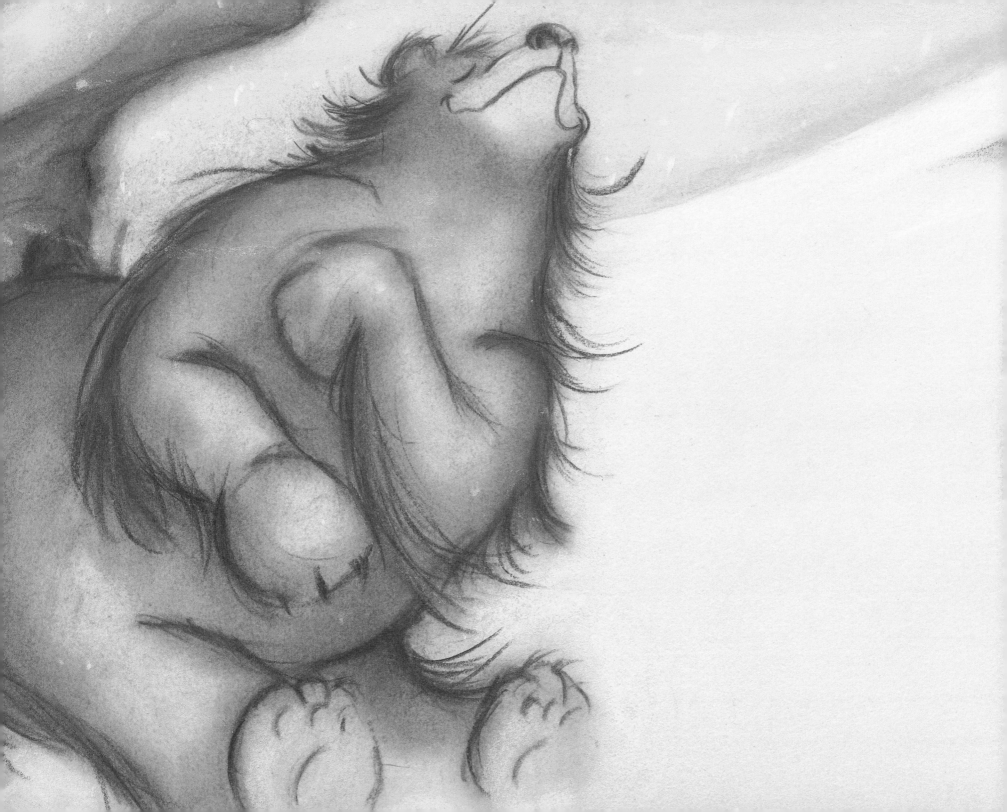

and old big as a boulder bear
crawls deep into his cave.
He settles his big bear body down,
all covered up
by his bearskin coat,

all wrapped up
in his big hairy bearskin coat,

except

for his no-hair nose.

A very hairy bear
DOES care
about ice cold air
on his no-hair nose,

especially

when he's sleepy.

So,

he puts his big warm
bearpaws,

his shaggy, raggy,
very hairy
bearpaws
on top of his nose,

and goes

to sleep.